HARD HAT AREA

SUSAN L. ROTH

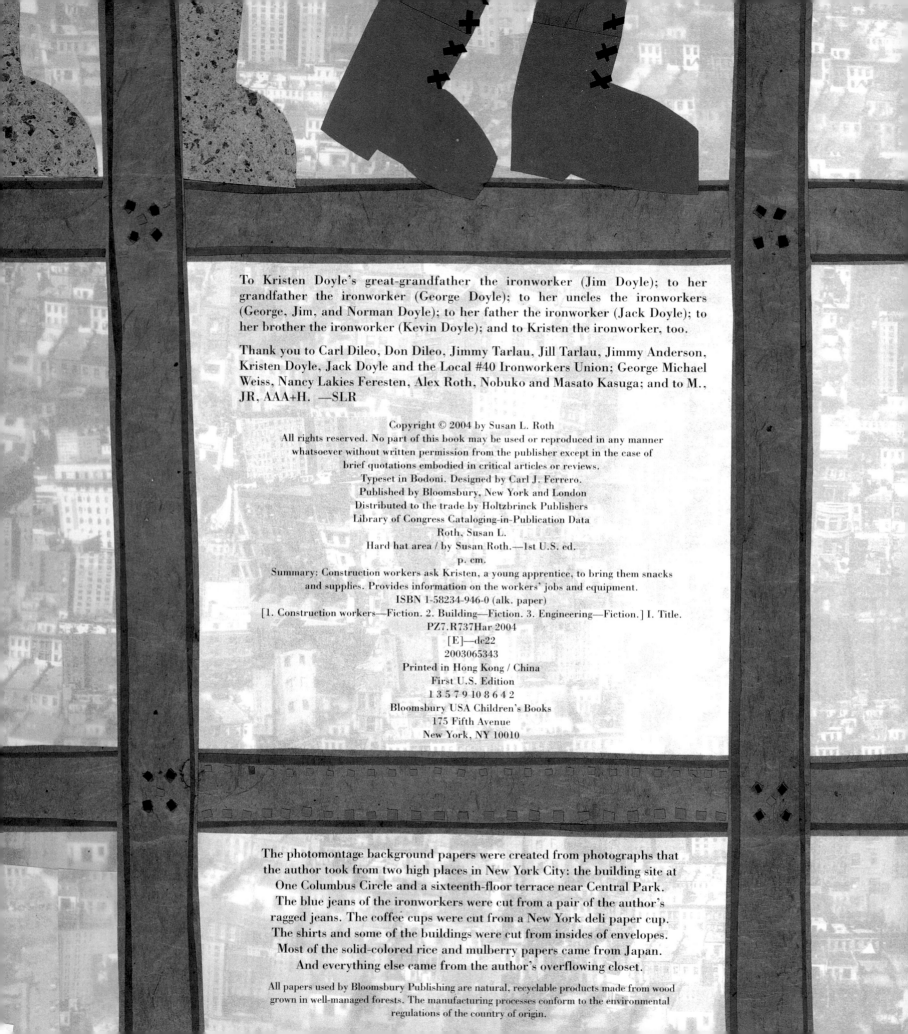

To Kristen Doyle's great-grandfather the ironworker (Jim Doyle); to her grandfather the ironworker (George Doyle); to her uncles the ironworkers (George, Jim, and Norman Doyle); to her father the ironworker (Jack Doyle); to her brother the ironworker (Kevin Doyle); and to Kristen the ironworker, too.

Thank you to Carl Dileo, Don Dileo, Jimmy Tarlau, Jill Tarlau, Jimmy Anderson, Kristen Doyle, Jack Doyle and the Local #40 Ironworkers Union; George Michael Weiss, Nancy Lakies Feresten, Alex Roth, Nobuko and Masato Kasuga; and to M., JR, AAA+H. —SLR

Copyright © 2004 by Susan L. Roth
Typeset in Bodoni. Designed by Carl J. Ferrero.
Published by Bloomsbury, New York and London
Distributed to the trade by Holtzbrinck Publishers
Library of Congress Cataloging-in-Publication Data
Roth, Susan L.
Hard hat area / by Susan Roth.—1st U.S. ed.
p. cm.
Summary: Construction workers ask Kristen, a young apprentice, to bring them snacks and supplies. Provides information on the workers' jobs and equipment.
ISBN 1-58234-946-0 (alk. paper)
[1. Construction workers—Fiction. 2. Building—Fiction. 3. Engineering—Fiction.] I. Title.
PZ7.R737Har 2004
[E]—dc22
2003065343
Printed in Hong Kong / China
First U.S. Edition
1 3 5 7 9 10 8 6 4 2
Bloomsbury USA Children's Books
175 Fifth Avenue
New York, NY 10010

The photomontage background papers were created from photographs that the author took from two high places in New York City: the building site at One Columbus Circle and a sixteenth-floor terrace near Central Park. The blue jeans of the ironworkers were cut from a pair of the author's ragged jeans. The coffee cups were cut from a New York deli paper cup. The shirts and some of the buildings were cut from insides of envelopes. Most of the solid-colored rice and mulberry papers came from Japan. And everything else came from the author's overflowing closet.

All papers used by Bloomsbury Publishing are natural, recyclable products made from wood grown in well-managed forests. The manufacturing processes conform to the environmental regulations of the country of origin.

HARD HAT AREA

SUSAN L. ROTH

BLOOMSBURY
CHILDREN'S
BOOKS

Kristen is an apprentice ironworker at a big building site. It is her job to help the men and women working there, bringing them tools, food, and drinks. As she works, she learns to be comfortable walking around way up high on the building. This is the story of one of her usual days.

As always, she is wearing her hard hat, her overalls, and her heavy lace-up boots. Thick gloves are in her pocket. She has her pencil and her pad. She is ready for work.

1   hard hat: worn to protect ironworkers' heads from falling objects or bumps; it is the law to wear a hard hat

2   overalls or pants without cuffs: prevent hot sparks from startling or burning the ironworker; keep ironworkers from tripping

3   heavy boots: protect feet from burns, welding sparks, mud, snow, and other things

4   lumphammer: used for hammering in small nails, called bullpins or driftpins, and for lining up the decking

5   site fence: goes around the construction site to keep out people who aren't working there

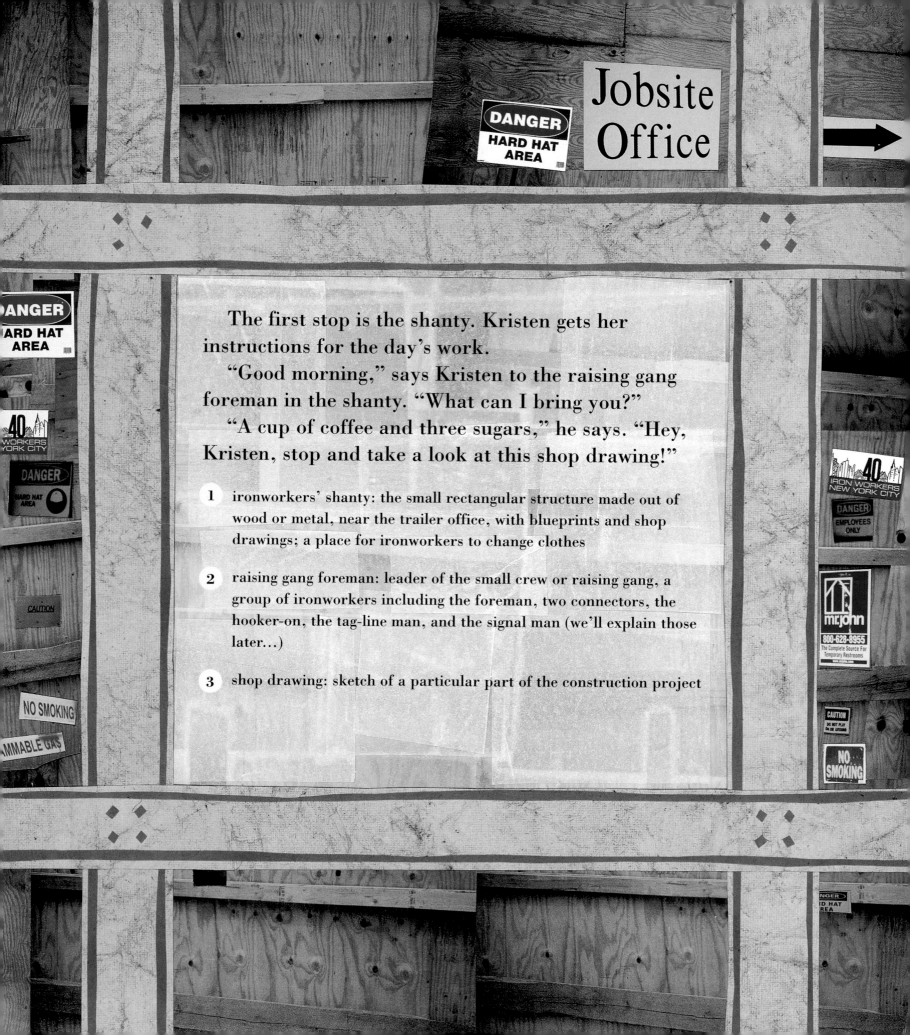

The first stop is the shanty. Kristen gets her instructions for the day's work.

"Good morning," says Kristen to the raising gang foreman in the shanty. "What can I bring you?"

"A cup of coffee and three sugars," he says. "Hey, Kristen, stop and take a look at this shop drawing!"

1 ironworkers' shanty: the small rectangular structure made out of wood or metal, near the trailer office, with blueprints and shop drawings; a place for ironworkers to change clothes

2 raising gang foreman: leader of the small crew or raising gang, a group of ironworkers including the foreman, two connectors, the hooker-on, the tag-line man, and the signal man (we'll explain those later...)

3 shop drawing: sketch of a particular part of the construction project

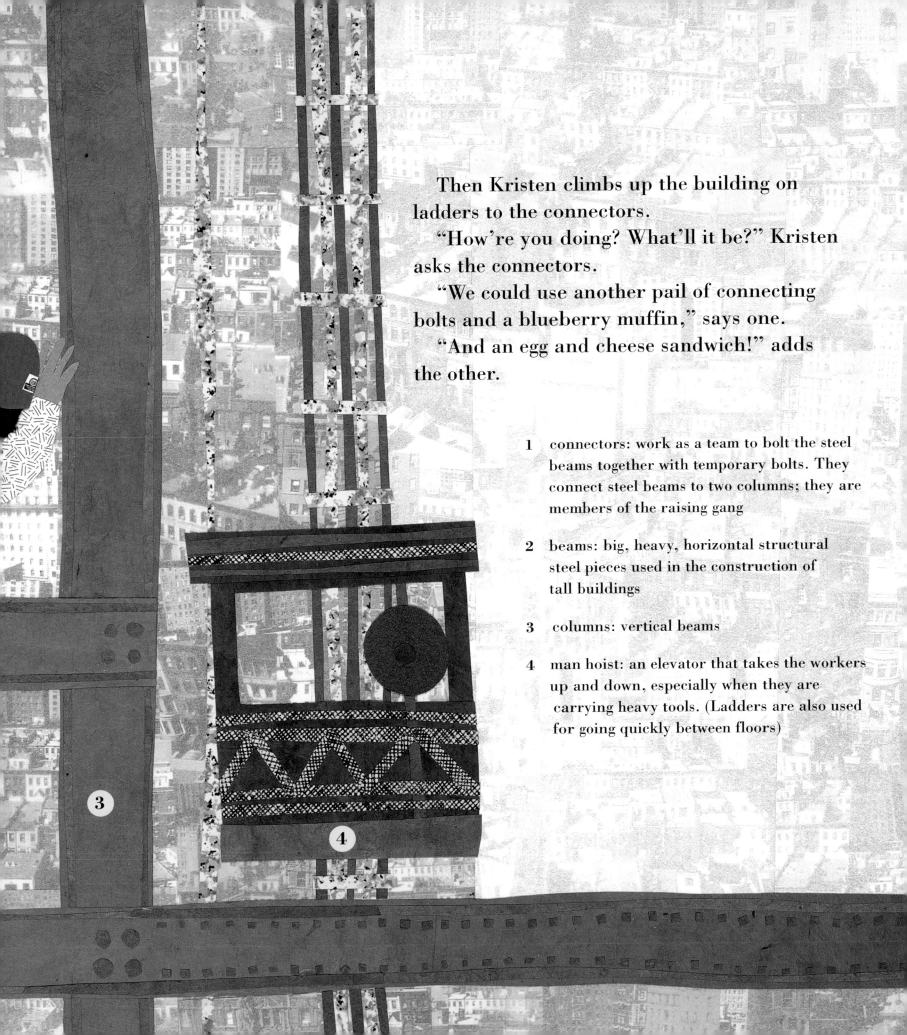

Then Kristen climbs up the building on ladders to the connectors.

"How're you doing? What'll it be?" Kristen asks the connectors.

"We could use another pail of connecting bolts and a blueberry muffin," says one.

"And an egg and cheese sandwich!" adds the other.

1   connectors: work as a team to bolt the steel beams together with temporary bolts. They connect steel beams to two columns; they are members of the raising gang

2   beams: big, heavy, horizontal structural steel pieces used in the construction of tall buildings

3   columns: vertical beams

4   man hoist: an elevator that takes the workers up and down, especially when they are carrying heavy tools. (Ladders are also used for going quickly between floors)

"Hello, hello," says Kristen to the hooker-on.
"Are you getting hungry?"

"I'm always hungry," he says. "Would you bring me a big hot chocolate, three oatmeal cookies, and a choker cable, too? I'll need another for my next load."

1. hooker-on: puts the choker cable around the iron beam to make it secure and balanced; a member of the raising gang

2. choker cable: very strong metal rope with secure loops on either end. It attaches to a hook, which is in turn attached to another cable, and then to the crane

3. heavy gloves: protect the workers' hands from getting hurt

"How's it going? What can I get you?"
Kristen asks the signal man.

"I could use some batteries for this telephone
and a big iced tea with lemon," he says.

1   signal man: communicates by telephone with the crane
    operator, giving him directions about which way to move
    his heavy iron load; a member of the raising gang

2   telephone: the workers all have phones to talk to each other
    from different parts of the building site

3   tower: this structure holds the crane

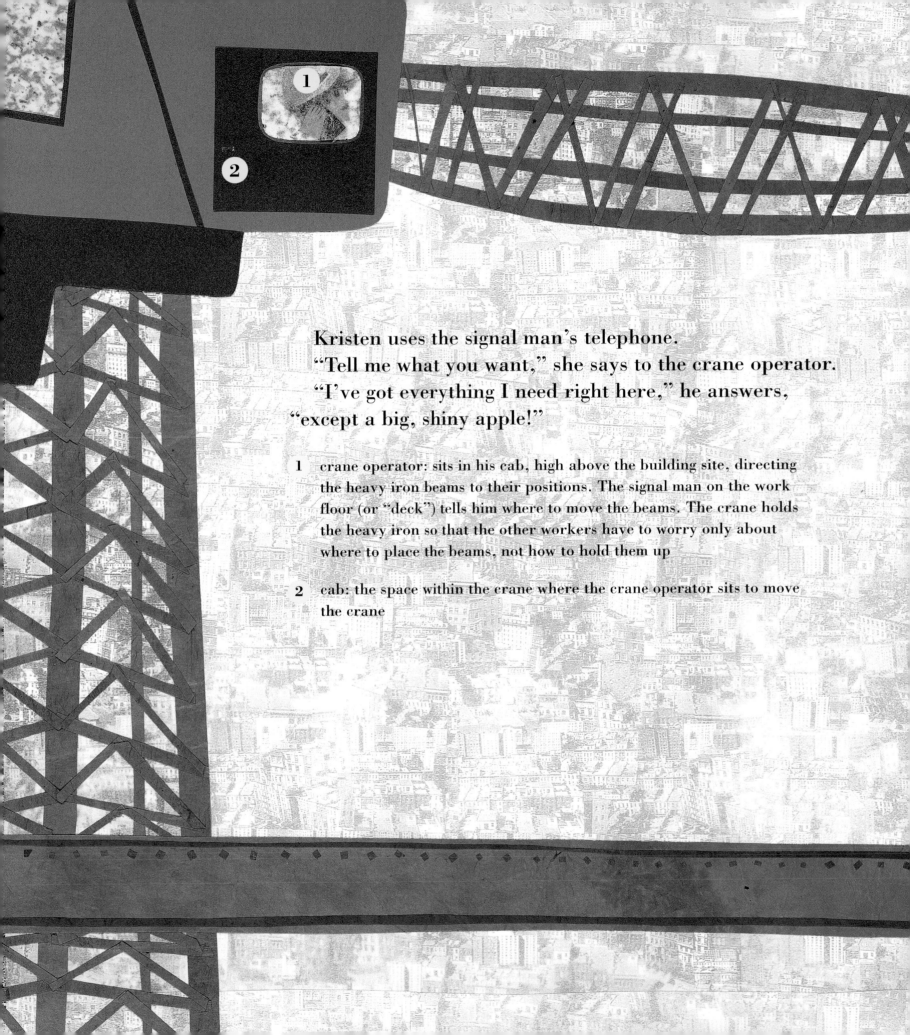

Kristen uses the signal man's telephone.
"Tell me what you want," she says to the crane operator.
"I've got everything I need right here," he answers,
"except a big, shiny apple!"

1   crane operator: sits in his cab, high above the building site, directing
     the heavy iron beams to their positions. The signal man on the work
     floor (or "deck") tells him where to move the beams. The crane holds
     the heavy iron so that the other workers have to worry only about
     where to place the beams, not how to hold them up

2   cab: the space within the crane where the crane operator sits to move
     the crane

"It's a beautiful day!" says Kristen to the plumber upper. "What'll you have?"

"Coffee, cream and sugar, and a bag of peanuts," he answers. "Check the bubble in the little window of my level. When it's right in the middle, this column will be straight up and down."

1   plumber upper: the person whose job it is to make everything stand straight, exactly square, up and down. "Plumb" means straight up and down, or vertical

2   level: the tool that shows when a column is perfectly perpendicular to (exactly upright from) the floor, like this: ⊥

3   spud wrenches: the most common tool of iron workers; used to tighten bolts. The long, pointy end is used to do many things, like lining up the holes made for the bolts

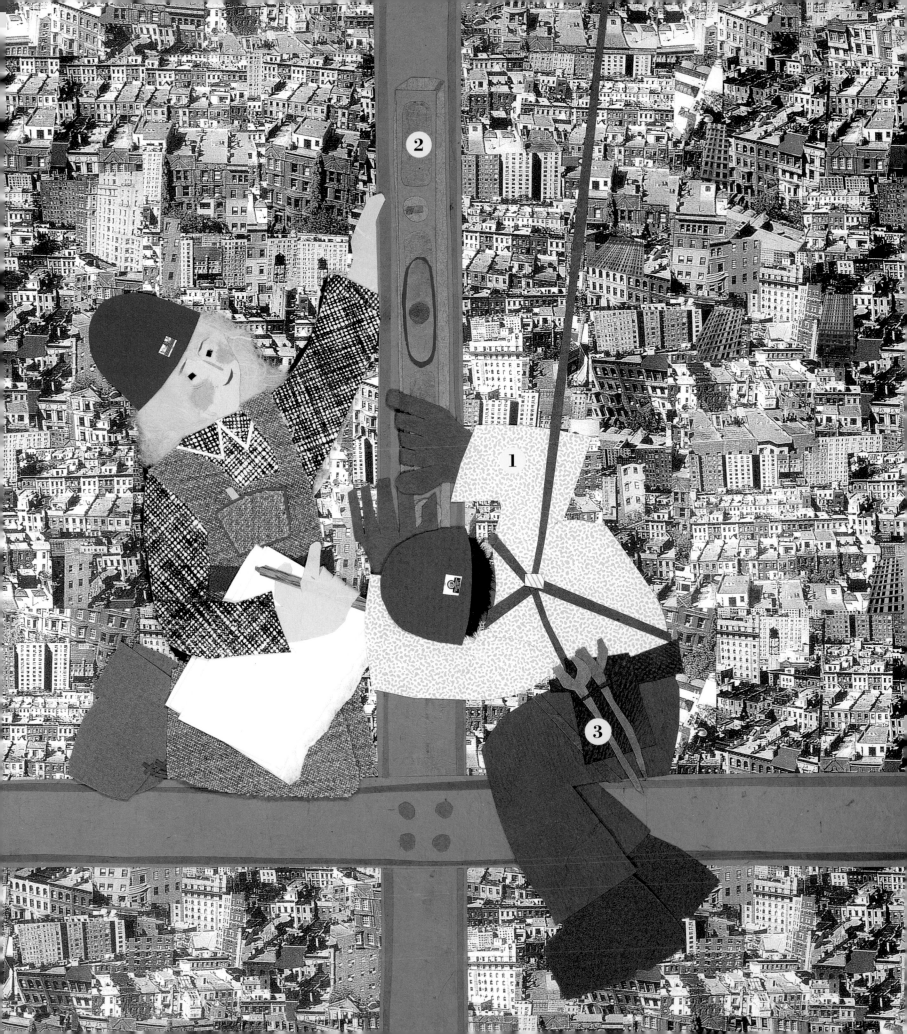

"Hey, what's happening?" Kristen asks the bolter upper. "What would you like?"

"I'm all set with my spud wrenches," she tells Kristen, "but I'd love a lemonade!"

1 bolter upper: installs and tightens the bolts after the connectors line up the beams

2 bolts: big, strong screws that hold beams in place

3 long sleeves: the workers try to wear them so they don't burn or cut themselves

4 braces: diagonal beams

"Ready for a snack?" Kristen asks the welder.
"I sure am!" he says. "Two bags of pretzels and a peppermint, please, and would you pick up a clear glass for my welding shield? I can hardly see through this one anymore."

1   welder: attaches (welds) metals together by heating and softening them with a welding torch

2   welding shield: heavy mask with a see-through window, worn by the welder to protect his face from flying sparks while allowing him to see what he is doing

3   welding torch: a tool that creates enough heat to soften metal

4   welder's sleeves: made of fireproof suede or leather to protect the welder from getting burned

"You must be starving by now!" says Kristen to the decker. "I bet you want six doughnuts."

"I'll settle for two if they're chocolate," he says. "And after the break, I'll need a box of welding rods—they hold the decking to the beams. Get someone to help you because they're heavy."

Now Kristen is ready to go back down to the ground.

1 decker: attaches the metal flooring (decking) onto the steel beams

2 decking: wide-grooved (corrugated) iron sheets used for flooring

3 lumphammer: the decker uses this to align the decking (Kristen has one, too)

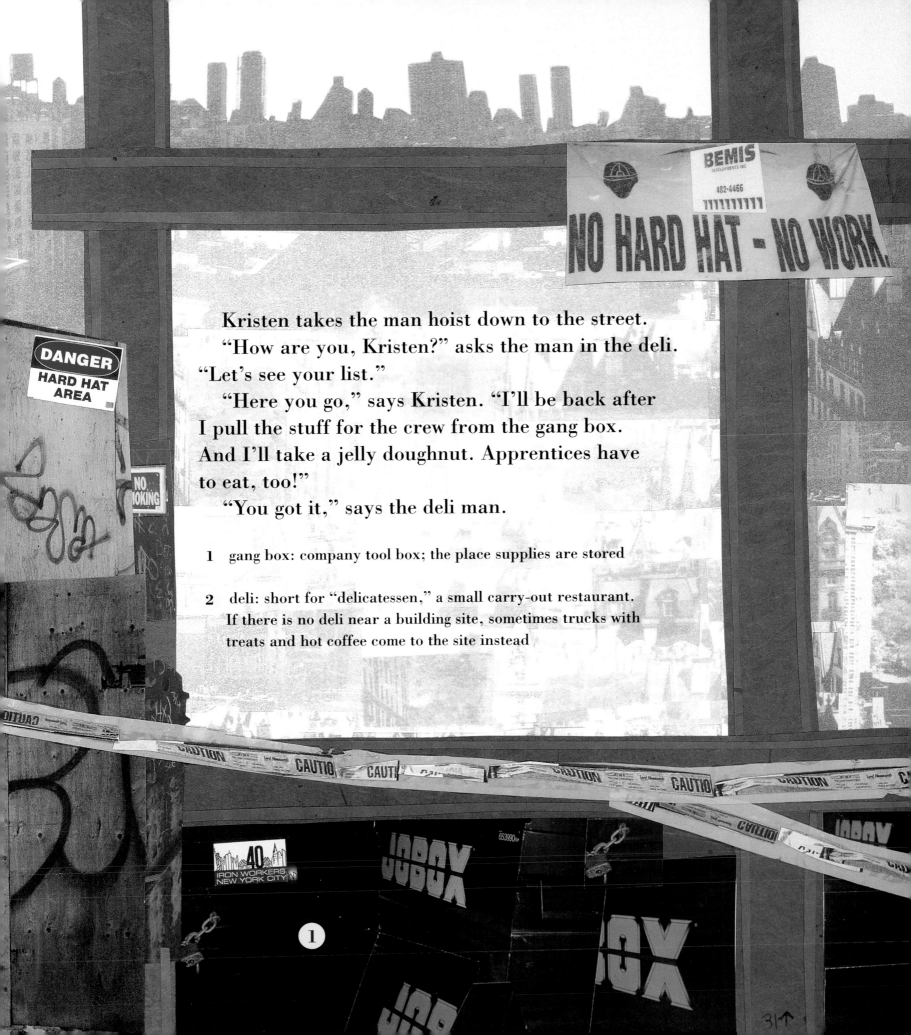

Kristen takes the man hoist down to the street.

"How are you, Kristen?" asks the man in the deli. "Let's see your list."

"Here you go," says Kristen. "I'll be back after I pull the stuff for the crew from the gang box. And I'll take a jelly doughnut. Apprentices have to eat, too!"

"You got it," says the deli man.

1   gang box: company tool box; the place supplies are stored

2   deli: short for "delicatessen," a small carry-out restaurant. If there is no deli near a building site, sometimes trucks with treats and hot coffee come to the site instead

When they get their snacks, the raising gang foreman, the connectors, the hooker-on, the tag-line man, the signal man, the crane operator, the plumber upper, the bolter upper, the welder, the decker, and Kristen, the apprentice, stop to eat.

1 building site: the whole area under construction, usually blocked off from the rest of the city by boards and yellow ribbons that say CAUTION! and DANGER!

BEMIS
DEVELOPMENTS INC
482-4466

And then they go
back to work.

Do you know
who's who?*

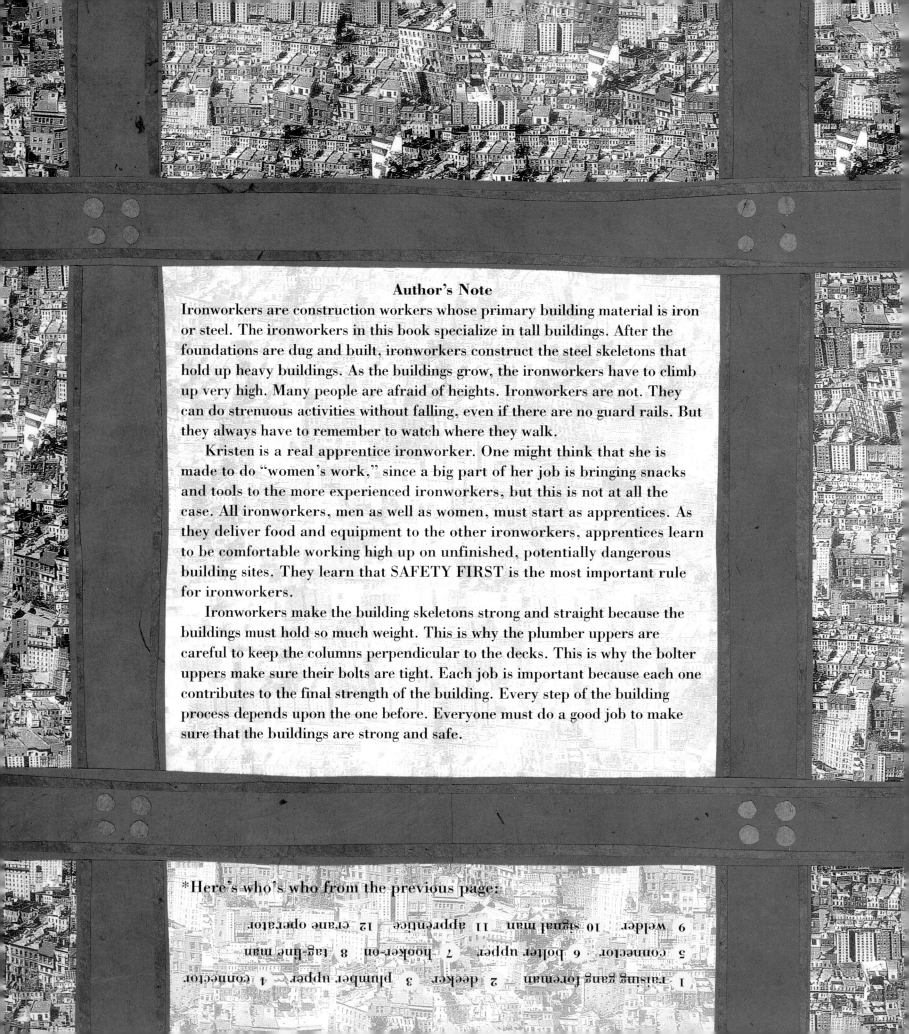

Author's Note

Ironworkers are construction workers whose primary building material is iron or steel. The ironworkers in this book specialize in tall buildings. After the foundations are dug and built, ironworkers construct the steel skeletons that hold up heavy buildings. As the buildings grow, the ironworkers have to climb up very high. Many people are afraid of heights. Ironworkers are not. They can do strenuous activities without falling, even if there are no guard rails. But they always have to remember to watch where they walk.

Kristen is a real apprentice ironworker. One might think that she is made to do "women's work," since a big part of her job is bringing snacks and tools to the more experienced ironworkers, but this is not at all the case. All ironworkers, men as well as women, must start as apprentices. As they deliver food and equipment to the other ironworkers, apprentices learn to be comfortable working high up on unfinished, potentially dangerous building sites. They learn that SAFETY FIRST is the most important rule for ironworkers.

Ironworkers make the building skeletons strong and straight because the buildings must hold so much weight. This is why the plumber uppers are careful to keep the columns perpendicular to the decks. This is why the bolter uppers make sure their bolts are tight. Each job is important because each one contributes to the final strength of the building. Every step of the building process depends upon the one before. Everyone must do a good job to make sure that the buildings are strong and safe.

*Here's who's who from the previous page:

1 raising gang foreman   2 decker   3 plumber upper   4 connector
5 connector   6 bolter upper   7 hooker-on   8 tag-line man
9 welder   10 signal man   11 apprentice   12 crane operator